Museum Mystery

Story by Diana Noonan

Illustrations by Miriam Serafin

Contents

Chapter 1

Out of Focus

Tick, tick, tick. Ella sat at her desk and stared at the clock on the classroom wall. It was Friday afternoon, and the air in the classroom was *stifling*. She couldn't wait for the clock to show 3 pm, so that she could go home and jump into the refreshing cool water of the spa pool with her brothers.

Around her, all Ella's classmates were silently reading their library books. At the front of the room, her teacher, Mr Snell, was reading *his* library book. At least, that's what Ella *thought* he was doing, but he seemed to know she wasn't concentrating, because he suddenly looked up at her and raised an eyebrow. It was his silent way of asking her to focus.

Ella looked down at the graphic novel lying open on her desk. RED (Read Every Day) had been going for fifteen minutes, and she hadn't even read one page. It was always the same – she just couldn't focus. Whenever she looked at words on a page, her mind would start thinking of a million different things. Like what her pet rabbit had been doing at home all day, or who she was going to invite to her birthday sleepover. Sometimes she thought about how much she loved dance class. Sometimes she just thought about the Moon and the stars, and if a spaceship would ever visit Earth.

It was the same whenever she had to write something, or give a presentation to the class. No matter how hard she tried, she just *couldn't* make her brain stay still long enough to focus on what she wanted to say, or write, or read.

Ella turned the next page in her book loudly, so that Mr Snell would hear it and think she *was* reading. Then she kept her head down until ten more minutes had passed and Mr Snell announced RED was over for the day.

"Take out your tablets, please," he said, "and open your writing folder. In it, you'll find the conservation report you wrote on a native animal, and you'll see that I've made some comments."

Mr Snell looked at Ella's friend Kenji. "Have you *actually* helped to put tags on saltwater crocodiles, Kenji?" asked Mr Snell, raising his eyebrows in disbelief. "A report is generally considered to be a piece of *non-fiction* writing!"

Kenji laughed. So did everyone else. But Ella wasn't laughing when she looked at the comments Mr Snell had made on her report. They were the same as always: "Good effort on the few paragraphs, Ella, but the report isn't finished. Try to focus, so that you don't run out of time."

But before Ella had time to feel too sorry for herself, Mr Snell said he had something exciting to tell the class. He asked them to turn off their tablets and listen carefully.

"In two weeks' time, we'll be going on a school camp," he said.

There was a rumble of excitement, and everyone began whispering to each other.

"This year, we're not going to be in tents, or even anywhere rural. We're going on a city camp and will stay at School Lodge in Harford."

Harford was just over an hour away. Most families only went there if they wanted to buy something special, or to see a show. Mr Snell continued. "Each morning, we'll be going to the museum to learn about how they research and build their displays."

"Palaeontology displays?" asked Ella's friend Daisy, who wanted to be an archaeologist someday.

"I'm not sure if there will be dinosaur exhibits at the museum or not," replied Mr Snell. "I guess we'll find out."

"What are we going to do in the afternoons?" asked Ella.

"From Monday to Thursday, we'll be doing a different activity each day," said Mr Snell. "On Friday, we'll spend all day at the museum. So far, our afternoon activities include the city hydro pool, an indoor rock-climbing centre and a historic railway park. I'll know more next week."

Before anyone could ask another question, the end-of-school bell rang loudly in the corridor outside the classroom, and Mr Snell began collecting the class's tablets.

"Have a good weekend, everyone!" he said, as the class filed out of the door.

Chapter 2

Snap!

As Ella walked home from school, she felt so excited about the city camp that she forgot all about Mr Snell's comments on her animal report, and about not being able to focus at RED time. And as soon as she heard her brothers splashing about in the spa, all she could think about was hopping into the cool water!

She was just about to call out to them to leave some water in the pool when she spotted Nan's car parked outside the house.

"I didn't know you were coming to visit!" said Ella, as she ran inside and found Nan sitting at the kitchen table, talking to Mum.

Nan gave Ella an affectionate hug. "I didn't know either!" she said. "But it's university holidays, and I thought, why not surprise you all!"

Ella's nan was a physics professor at the university, three hours' drive away, and Ella would sometimes go to her place for a break in the school holidays.

"How was class today?" Mum asked Ella.

"We're going on camp!" replied Ella. "To Harford!"

"Oh," said Nan, "a city camp! That's different."

Ella told Mum and Nan everything Mr Snell had said.

"And how was RED?" asked Mum.

Ella pulled a chair back from the table and collapsed into it, dramatically. "Same as always," she complained.

Mum passed Ella a glass of lemon water. "Next month, we're going to see the learning specialist your teacher recommended," she reminded her. "Mr Snell thinks she can help."

Ella sighed. "I *hope* so. We have to do so much reading and writing on our own this year, rather than in groups. It's so hard to focus on silent reading and report writing! I don't think my brain works like everyone else's."

"Snap!" said Nan, looking at Ella. "I was just the same. I could never focus on my reading and writing when I was at school, and I also found it difficult to concentrate when someone was explaining something to me. When I look back, I don't think there was very much I *could* focus on!"

Ella nodded. "That's *exactly* what it's like for me!" she said.

"I must have been quite imaginative, though," added Nan, "because my mind would wander in all sorts of rather interesting directions."

"But you're a university professor, Nan," said Ella. "So you must have been brilliant at schoolwork."

"I only experienced success once I found a subject I was extremely interested in," said Nan with a smile.

"Physics?" asked Ella.

"That's right," said Nan. "One day, our teacher asked us to design a see-saw that a monkey and an elephant could play on together – one at each end."

"A monkey *and* an elephant on the same see-saw? That would be impossible!" said Ella.

"Not if the see-saw was designed in a rather smart way," smiled Nan. "Anyway, I wanted to design that see-saw so much that I taught myself how to focus on reading and maths."

"Mm," said Ella, as she sipped her lemon water. "I hope that happens to me."

"I'm sure the learning specialist will help you find ways to make schoolwork easier, too," said Nan. "But for me, discovering something I was really interested in was the *best* way to focus that I ever found."

Chapter 3

A Cardboard Conversation

The next two weeks went by very quickly as Ella's class prepared for camp. There were meals to plan, venues to research, emails to write, lists to make and bags to pack. Before they knew it, the class was in the school bus on the way to the city.

"I hope we get to share the same bunk room," said Daisy, who was in the seat beside Ella.

"I hope the museum sessions are fun," replied Ella.

But later, as she scrambled off the bus at the museum and headed through its wide glass doors, Ella's stomach was churning. What if the sessions required a lot of reading and writing, and she couldn't do the work because she couldn't focus? Before she had time to think any more about it, a museum education officer was waving them over to the reception area.

"My name is Ms Nulgit," she said, introducing herself to the class.

Ms Nulgit led Ella and her classmates upstairs to a long, echoey hall on the first floor of the building. It was lined with brightly lit bays, each the size of a small bedroom, and in each bay was a display.

"This floor of the museum is all about Harford's history," explained Ms Nulgit, as the class sat down on a cluster of chairs and beanbags in the middle of the hall. "Each display represents a different aspect of the life that was once lived here. There are displays about First Nations peoples, colonial settlement, farming, fishing, rope making, gold mining, shops and schools."

"So, not so much about palaeontology, then?" asked Mr Snell, glancing at Daisy.

"Not so far," said Ms Nulgit, with a laugh. "But we're always discovering new information, so one day there might be!"

Ms Nulgit gave everyone a pen and a clipboard with a piece of paper on it. Then she explained what she wanted the class to do.

"At the top of your clipboard is the name of the display I want you to find," Ms Nulgit said. "You have ten minutes to study the display and write down five pieces of information you learn from it."

"*Cool!*" Ella heard Kenji say, but she was already worrying about how she would be able to read and write quickly enough to complete the task in just ten minutes.

"Off you go!" said Ms Nulgit. "I've set my stopwatch."

Ella saw "Gold Mining" written at the top of her paper. She walked quickly around the hall until she found the gold mining display. Kenji was already standing in front of it, talking to Mr Snell and Marko and Lexi, two other kids from Ella's class.

"Did you know that Harford was once a gold mining settlement?" Mr Snell asked Ella, as she joined the group.

Ella shook her head.

"That was a hundred and fifty years ago," said Mr Snell. "In those days, it was called 'Canvas Town', because of all the canvas tents the gold miners used as their temporary homes. See what you can learn about Canvas Town, everyone. And remember, you don't have to *read* everything to find out information. You can learn a lot by looking at the photos, models and objects on display."

Ella nodded. She knew Mr Snell was trying to help her.

After he'd walked away to talk to some other students, Ella looked hard at the display. A sagging green tent dominated, and beside it was an old shovel and pick leaning against a pile of rocks. A gold pan lay beside a sparkling, artificial stream. But what Ella noticed more than anything else was the life-sized cut-out cardboard figure of a boy her own age. It had been constructed from a photo of a real person.

The boy's face was grubby, and so were his long-sleeved shirt and thick vest. A pair of suspenders held up his trousers, and his curly hair was half-hidden by a cap. Rather than being unable to focus, which was what usually happened within a few minutes of her trying to concentrate on anything, Ella couldn't stop staring at the expression on the boy's face. He looked deeply sad and worried, but there was something else in his eyes that Ella couldn't quite identify.

"I've got my five points," she heard Kenji say. "Do you want me to help you get yours, Ella?"

But Ella didn't answer. She was still studying the boy's face, and, in a way that felt very unsettling, she felt he was also studying her.

"What's his name?" she heard herself ask.

"He's Danny Brown," said Kenji. "See, there's a label down by his feet. It says 'Danny Brown, station master's son'."

Before she could reply, Ella heard Ms Nulgit calling the class back to the seats in the middle of the hall. Kenji walked away with Marko and Lexi, but Ella stayed where she was, as if glued to the spot.

"Now what am I going to do?" Ella wondered, looking at Danny. "I haven't written anything down!"

Danny looked straight back at her, and it felt to Ella as if he was holding her there with his gaze, pleading with her to stay. Or, was he trying to tell her something? She felt a chill run down her back.

"I *have* to go," she told him quickly, then checked herself. Why was she talking to a cardboard cut-out?

Chapter 4

Ella Speaks Out

Ms Nulgit went round the class, asking everyone to read out one point they had written down from their display observations. When she got to Ella, Ella felt her face redden.

"It's okay, Ella," said Mr Snell, quickly. "You can tell us something you learnt, even if you didn't write it down."

"Well," said Ella, feeling grateful to Mr Snell, "Danny, the boy in the gold mining display, is worried about something. And he's sad. You can tell by the look on his face."

"You're very observant to realise that," said Ms Nulgit. "He *is* worried. It's because his father, Robert Brown, has been sent to prison."

Ella gasped.

"Mr Brown was Canvas Town's part-time station master," continued Ms Nulgit. "He also had a small gold mining claim – that's a piece of land where he had the right to search for gold. It was on the edge of town."

Kenji put up his hand.

"Yes?" said Ms Nulgit.

Kenji looked at the points he had written on his clipboard.

"One day, Mr Brown didn't do his job properly," Kenji said. "He forgot to set the train signal to 'stop' and it caused a train crash."

"People said he had 'gold fever'," added Marko, reading from his own clipboard. "They said all Mr Brown could think about was gold, and that's why he rushed off to his claim without doing his station master job properly."

"That's not true!" said a voice behind Ella.

She spun round and looked across at the gold mining display on the far wall of the hall.

"Tell them it's not true!" said the voice again. Ella wasn't sure if it was a voice that anyone else could hear, because it felt as if it was echoing inside her head.

"He *did* set the signal to 'stop'!" said the voice, and now Ella was *sure* it came from the cardboard cut-out. Before she knew what was happening, her hand was in the air, and she was waving it to get Ms Nulgit's attention.

"Yes?" asked Ms Nulgit.

"That's not right," said Ella. "What Kenji and Marko said about the station master – it isn't true. He did set the signal to 'stop'."

A puzzled expression came over Ms Nulgit's face, and she looked at Ella curiously.

"If you read the text in the display, I think you'll find he didn't," Ms Nulgit said. "Mr Brown's error caused the train to hit a wagon that was parked further along the track. As a consequence, the train driver was seriously injured and spent several months in hospital. The signal was still on 'go' from when the train had passed through the day before."

"Tell her! Tell her it wasn't my father's fault!" Danny's words hissed like a whisper in Ella's ear.

"No," said Ella, slowly shaking her head. "It wasn't Mr Brown's fault."

"Ella!" said Mr Snell, firmly. "I think Ms Nulgit would know."

"I do," nodded Ms Nulgit, looking disturbed and a little annoyed. "I worked on the display myself. This is the first day it's been open to the public."

Ella didn't know what to say, and now everyone in the class was staring at her.

"Sorry," she said quietly, shuffling her feet. "I must have got it wrong."

For the rest of the morning, Ella didn't say another word. When the class went on a tour of the transport display on the next floor, she kept to herself.

"I'm pleased we didn't come to Harford on *that*!" joked Mr Snell, as he pointed to an old bus that had a long snout of an engine and no windows.

Everyone laughed, but all Ella wanted to do was to return to the old mining display. How could a cardboard cut-out speak? And why did it speak to *her*?

"It can't have," she told herself. "I must have imagined it."

But she knew she hadn't.

Chapter 5

Danny Speaks Again

Back in the city history hall, Ms Nulgit was waiting for them.

"Great work today, everyone," she said. "I'm looking forward to seeing you all again tomorrow morning!"

"What will we be doing?" asked Daisy.

"You'll be starting work on a display of your own!" explained Ms Nulgit.

"A display about what?" asked Kenji.

"Cliffton!" said Ms Nulgit. "Your town may be an hour away, but we have everything here to help you research it – old photos, diaries, recorded stories and artefacts."

"What are artefacts?" asked Kenji.

"They're objects from the past," said Ms Nulgit. "Your museum in Cliffton isn't big enough to look after most of the artefacts and other historical records that have been found in that area. It also doesn't have the special storage rooms needed to take care of them. So, most items are kept safely here, at the city museum."

"Making our own display – that sounds like fun!" Kenji whispered to Ella.

Ella nodded. Now that she was back in the city history hall, and Danny was silent, she was feeling happier. She decided she really *had* imagined the cardboard cut-out speaking to her.

The class started following Mr Snell downstairs, but as Ella was about to join them, something made her glance back.

Ms Nulgit was standing beside the gold mining display, with her hands on her hips, studying it closely. Suddenly, Ella heard the voice again. This time, there was no mistaking it. It was the voice of a boy her own age, and it was coming from the cardboard cut-out of Danny.

"Help me!" Ella heard him say. "Please, help me, Ella!"

She gasped. Danny knew her name! She opened her mouth to say something back to him, then thought better of it.

"Come on, Ella!" called Daisy from the top of the stairs. "Or the bus will go without you!"

That afternoon, after the class had settled into School Lodge, and everyone had eaten lunch in the long dining hall, they boarded the bus again for the city hydro park.

"It's cool that we're in the same bunk room!" Daisy said to Ella, as they pulled on their swimsuits in the park's changing rooms. "I've got some new graphic novels. We can read them together!"

"Okay," said Ella quietly.

She took a quick shower, then followed the other girls out to the pool.

Although she joined in with everyone else as they zipped down the water slides and surfed on bodyboards in the churning wave pool, Ella couldn't stop thinking about the mysterious voice at the museum. She wished she could tell someone about it, but she just didn't know where to begin.

And if she thought things were going to get better, she was wrong. The trouble was just beginning, and it started as soon as the class arrived at the museum the following morning.

Chapter 6

Museum Detectives

"Welcome back," said Ms Nulgit with a smile, when Ella's class arrived at the museum on day two of their camp. "This morning, you'll be working in groups, and your first task is to decide what aspect of Cliffton's history your display will be about. Then, we'll help you research information about your chosen subject."

"Can a display be about the games Cliffton kids played a hundred years ago?" asked Lexi.

"Absolutely!" said Ms Nulgit. "That's a great suggestion."

"How about Cliffton's first sport clubs?" asked Marko, enthusiastically.

"Yes," said Ms Nulgit. "We have a lot of material in our collection about that subject."

Suddenly, everyone was coming up with ideas. Mr Snell walked around the chairs. "What subject would you like to research?" he asked Ella.

"I'm going to research Mr Brown and the train accident," she said, although she didn't know where that idea had come from, or how the words had found their way out of her mouth. "I want to find out if it was really his fault."

"Ms Nulgit wants everyone to research something to do with *Cliffton*," said Mr Snell.

"The train accident!" said a voice. It seemed so loud and so real that Ella actually stood up so she could look over to the gold mining display and the cut-out of Danny.

"We're not quite ready to start," said Ms Nulgit, when she saw Ella getting up out of her seat.

"I'm *not* starting," replied Ella. "I just ... I just ..." she didn't know what to say.

"Let's leave the group for a quick chat," said Mr Snell, quietly, to Ella. He smiled at Ms Nulgit. "We'll be right back," he told her.

"I *have* to research the train accident," said Ella, when she and Mr Snell were standing a short distance away from the class.

Mr Snell opened his mouth to object, but Ella interrupted with an idea she thought might convince him.

"I want to learn more about the train accident because then I would feel like I was being a detective. And that would be so interesting that I *know* I could make myself focus on the research."

Mr Snell looked puzzled, and suddenly Ella found herself telling him all about Nan, and how it wasn't until she'd become really interested in the see-saw project that she had taught herself to focus on maths and reading.

Ella could tell Mr Snell was thinking about what she had said, and was taking her seriously.

"Well … all right," he said at last. "I'll talk to Ms Nulgit about your suggestion. But if she agrees, you'll have to convince at least two other classmates to join you. This project is about learning to work with others, too."

While Mr Snell went to talk to Ms Nulgit, Ella found Daisy and Kenji. She explained to them why she wanted them to join her group, but was careful not to mention anything about the voice she thought she'd heard. As she finished, Mr Snell came over.

"Ms Nulgit has agreed to your plan," he told Ella. "She likes the idea of a team of detectives making their own display!"

"Museum detectives!" said Daisy. "Okay," she told Ella. "I'll join you!"

"Me, too!" said Kenji. "But only because Ms Nulgit said the museum has nothing in its files about Cliffton crocodiles."

"That's because Cliffton doesn't have a lake or a river," said Mr Snell, laughing. "And last time I checked, there were no crocs in the school pool!"

Chapter 7

The Investigation Begins

"Tell us again why you think the train accident wasn't Mr Brown's fault," Daisy said to Ella, when the three of them were sitting at a desk in a research room in the basement of the museum.

Ella and Daisy were carefully turning the pages of two old newspapers. Beside them, perched on a stool, Kenji was looking through a box of old sepia-coloured photos.

"It's because Danny – the boy in the gold mining display upstairs – looks so upset," said Ella, again being careful not to mention the voice she had heard.

"He looks sad and worried because his father went to prison," said Daisy.

"But he doesn't look *just* sad and worried," said Ella. "There's something else, too. You can see it in his eyes. It's as if he knows something unfair has happened."

"I don't understand how you can tell so much just by looking at his expression," said Daisy.

Ella wondered if she should try to explain the voice. But what if Daisy and Kenji didn't believe her and stopped wanting to help with the research?

"There were gold miners' tents everywhere!" said Kenji, interrupting her thoughts. "Look!" He held up a faded photo of a hillside covered in tents and huge piles of rock.

"You're supposed to be looking for photos of Mr Brown's gold claim," said Ella.

"I know," said Kenji, "but it's *all* so interesting."

"Same with the things in this old newspaper," said Daisy. She pointed to an advertisement for women's clothing. "Imagine having to wear all those petticoats!" She laughed. "You'd be so hot!"

Ella looked at the clock on the research room wall. It was almost time for lunch.

"We have to focus!" she told Kenji and Daisy. "We only have today and tomorrow to complete our research. Then we have to start work on the display."

Ella looked down at the article in front of her. It was about Mr Brown becoming the new station master. But even though she knew it was important that she read it, her mind still kept wandering. What would it be like to have her own father in prison, she wondered – and for something he hadn't done! What would people say about her family?

After a while, Ella found it helped if she put her finger under each word as she read it. That way, whenever her mind wandered, she could quickly return to the place she needed to start reading from again. A little later, she discovered that just holding her finger on the page was enough to remind her to focus on the words.

"Yes! I can *do* this!" she said, excitedly.

"Do what?" asked Kenji.

"Oh, did I say that out loud?" Ella giggled. "Sorry!"

Chapter 8

Time to Focus

That afternoon, on the rock climbing wall at the indoor activity centre, Ella put one hand in front of the other. Slowly and steadily, she carefully pulled herself up the wall with only rocks to hold on to and stand on. Even though she had a safety rope around her waist, she still felt nervous.

"You're doing really well!" shouted Lisa, the rock climbing instructor, who was holding the safety belay rope from below. "I can see you're focusing on where to put your hands as well as your feet."

There it was again – that word "focus", thought Ella, as she finally reached the top of the climb. And, for the first time, she began to think about what "focusing" actually meant. She was still thinking about it that night, as she climbed into bed.

"About our museum research," she said to Daisy, who was in the bunk above her, "I think it's important for us to focus on what we already have, rather than to keep searching for new information."

"I don't know what you mean," replied Daisy, leaning over the side to look at Ella.

"It's like rock climbing," Ella explained. "The foot- and handholds are already there. You just have to focus on finding them. And if you do, you'll eventually get to the top of the wall."

"Huh?" asked Daisy. "I don't get it."

"At the moment," continued Ella, "we're hoping to find out if Danny's father really did cause the train accident. We keep looking for new clues in a newspaper article or a report or a photo to help us do that. But maybe we already *have* the information we need, and we just need to focus on it to find the answer."

"Maybe you're right," said Daisy, although she sounded uncertain.

"I *think* I am," said Ella. "Let's talk about it with Kenji tomorrow."

Chapter 9

Ella Takes Note

On day three at the museum, Ella, Kenji and Daisy held a meeting in the basement research room. Ella explained the focusing idea to Kenji, who seemed to know what she meant.

"So," he said, "what we need to do now is to investigate more closely the information we already have, in case we've missed anything, and then link up everything we find."

"Yes," said Ella. "Let's stop researching and start focusing."

Daisy picked up a file containing sheets of paper. "These are the photocopies Ms Nulgit made for us," she said. "They're all of the newspaper articles we thought were important."

"And these are the photos we thought might help us," said Kenji, taking a lid off a box. He glanced up at the museum storage shelves. "But there are boxes of others I haven't even checked, yet."

Ella took a deep breath. "We haven't got time to look through any more of them," she said. "We have to focus and work with what we have – remember?"

Ella picked up a piece of paper and a pen. "You go first, Daisy," she said. "What have we found out from the old newspaper articles we've read?"

"Well," said Daisy, "Mr Brown didn't have to buy his gold claim. It was given to him by the railway company as part of his wages for being the station master. He was allowed to leave the station at 10 am each morning, after he'd set the signal for the train that would arrive in Canvas Town at midday."

Ella noted down the facts, forcing herself to focus on writing, even though she would rather have asked more questions.

"We also know that the train accident happened at 12:15 pm," said Daisy. "You found that out in a police report you read yesterday, Ella."

"That's right," said Ella, writing it down. "The accident happened because the signal was set at 'go' instead of 'stop', which is why the engine hit a wagon further down the line."

"If Mr Brown was telling the truth," said Kenji, "the station signal must have been set to 'stop' when he left for his gold mining claim after 10 am on the morning of the accident."

"But it must have been set to 'go' by the time the train arrived at the station at midday," said Ella.

"Maybe the train driver made a mistake," suggested Daisy. "Maybe he thought the signal said 'go', but it really said 'stop'."

"There were three people who saw the signal in the 'go' position that day," said Ella, reaching for one of the photocopied articles from the newspaper. "There was the train driver, his stoker, and a woman who walked past the station at 11:45 am. I read it in this police report. It said the woman's husband was panning in the river for gold, and she was taking him his lunch. She was surprised to see the signal in the 'go' position, because she had heard men were working further down the line, and she knew they usually parked a repair wagon on the track when they were doing that."

"But that seems to prove that Mr Brown *must* have made the mistake," said Kenji. He shook his head. "If only we could see back in time and find out for ourselves."

No one said anything – they were all too busy thinking hard.

"I'll re-check some of the photos I've already looked at, in case they show the signal," said Kenji.

"How would that help?" asked Daisy, impatiently. "It won't tell us the day the photo was taken, or at what *time* of day!"

"We don't have time to argue," said Ella, standing up. "You two keep going over the material we already have. I'm going back to the city history hall to look at the display again. I didn't really focus the first time I looked at it, and maybe I missed something."

"Sorry, Kenji," Ella heard Daisy say, as she left them. "I know you're doing your best. We all are. It's just so frustrating that we don't seem to be getting anywhere."

Chapter 10

Boldy-the-Bad

Out in the city history hall, the chairs and beanbags had been cleared away and desks were set up in their place. Ms Nulgit was introducing a tall young man to a couple of the other groups.

"This is Andre, our art director," she said. "If you have any questions about how to design your display, he's the person to consult!"

Ella winced. If the "detective team", as Ms Nulgit and Mr Snell had begun calling Ella, Daisy and Kenji, didn't start on their display soon, there wouldn't be enough time to get it finished.

Ella walked across to the gold mining display, where Danny was still staring out at her with his pleading eyes.

"I'm doing my best!" she hissed at him, even though he wasn't speaking to her today. Then she felt cross. "Why can't you *help* me instead of just standing there!" she told him.

For an instant, Ella thought she saw Danny's eyes move. It was as if he had tried to glance, for just a microsecond, at the wall behind him. She looked at the rear of the display.

"What is it?" she whispered to him. "What do you want me to notice?"

But Danny remained silent, as if all his energy had been used up in that brief movement of his eyes.

Ella found herself wanting to absorb everything on the rear wall at once, even though she knew she had to concentrate on one item at a time. But it was so difficult; everything kept running one into the other. One minute she was looking at the picks and shovels leaning against a pile of rocks, but before she could think about them, she was staring at an old boot, a sack hammock, a set of scales, or a blackened billycan hanging over a cooking fire. And accompanying it all was the background chatter and laughter of her classmates as they worked on their own displays.

Ella held up a hand on each side of her face so she could see only one small part of the gold mining display at a time. Then, she took a long, deep breath, did her best to ignore the noise in the hall, and focused with all her might on each and every item on the back wall. And, suddenly, she saw it!

It was a photo she hadn't even noticed before – and it was of an enormous bull. She could tell how large the bull was, because it was standing beside the Canvas Town railway station.

"What are you doing *there*?" she said out loud.

"Are you talking about the photo of the bull?" asked a voice beside her.

For a moment, Ella thought it was Danny who had spoken, but when she looked up, she found it was Ms Nulgit.

"Yes," said Ella. "He's huge. And he looks …"

"Scary?"

Ella nodded. "He's got wild eyes and he looks like he's pawing the ground – as if he might be going to charge!"

"My research on Canvas Town suggests he was a *very* wild bull," said Ms Nulgit. "And an exceptionally badly behaved one! The local miners nicknamed him 'Boldy' because he was so fearless."

"What did he do?" asked Ella.

"For a start," said Ms Nulgit, "if he heard a cow bellowing, he used to come bounding out of the bush around Canvas Town and chase after it. He used to chase any children who got in his way, too!"

"Wasn't he in a paddock with a fence around it?" asked Ella.

"No," said Ms Nulgit. "Apparently, he had escaped from his field when he was just a young animal, and run off into the bush. That's why he was so wild. And he was so strong and so fast, no one could ever catch him to pen him up again."

"But why is he in a gold mining display?" asked Ella.

"He's there because he used to come into the miners' camp at night, on his way from one place to another. He kept to the miners' trails, and he enjoyed scratching his back by rubbing against the piles of rocks the miners had stacked up. We know, from articles in the Canvas Town newspaper, that he would knock the rocks over and send them flying down the hill towards the tents where the men were sleeping."

Ella gasped. "So he was dangerous as well as badly behaved!" she said.

"He was," agreed Ms Nulgit. "He was a significant part of Canvas Town life, so we're lucky to have a photograph of him. In fact, we have several photos of Boldy, and, by coincidence, they were all taken on the day of the train accident."

"Really?" asked Ella. "How do you know?"

"The photographer who took them was a professional, called Abraham Scully," said Ms Nulgit. "And he always signed and dated the back of his images. Mr Scully used to travel from town to town, mainly taking family portraits. But he also took photos of the places he visited."

Ella nodded.

"His photos are a big part of why we know so much about Canvas Town, and they're one of the reasons we decided to make the display."

"So Boldy turned up at the railway station on the day of the train accident," said Ella, "and Mr Scully snapped some photos of him."

"That's right," said Ms Nulgit. "Boldy was a rather handsome beast, and had a bad reputation, so I'm not surprised Mr Scully was interested in him."

As Ella listened, she felt a prickling sensation at the back of her neck. What Ms Nulgit was saying was *extremely* important. If Mr Scully had taken *several* photos of Boldy at the railway station on the day of the accident, perhaps those same photos would also show what the signal was set to!

Ella's heart began to thump with excitement. But, a minute later, as she hurried back to the research room to tell Daisy and Kenji her news, she stopped dead in her tracks. Even if the photos *did* show the signal, they still wouldn't help solve the mystery, because there was no way of knowing the time of day that they were taken. They could have been snapped before or after Mr Brown left for the gold claim.

Ella was so disappointed, she wanted to cry.

But, back in the research room, Daisy and Kenji had made a discovery that would change everything!

Chapter 11

A Helpful Discovery

Kenji and Daisy were hunched over some photos when Ella returned to the research room. Their noses were almost touching the work bench. "We found this on one of the shelves," said Daisy, holding up a thick magnifying glass.

"We're using it to focus more closely on the photos," added Kenji.

"You try it!" said Daisy, passing the magnifying glass to Ella. "It's so powerful!"

Ella peered down through the magnifying glass at a photo lying on the bench in front of her of the Canvas Town railway station. Little by little she moved the glass over the image. Suddenly, she saw something that made her gasp.

"A clock!" she said. "There's a clock hanging down from the underside of the station's platform roof. *And* you can see what time it's showing!

"There was a professional photographer, called Mr Scully, working in Canvas Town on the morning of the train accident," Ella told Daisy and Kenji excitedly. "He took some photos of the railway station."

"Is that photo one of them?" asked Daisy.

"No," said Ella, showing them the back of the photo, which was blank. "Mr Scully always dated and signed the back of his photos. But if we can find the ones he took of the station that morning, and they show the signal set to 'stop' after 10 am, then we'd know that Mr Brown told the truth!"

"What are we waiting for?" said Kenji, reaching up to the shelves for the remaining boxes of Canvas Town photos. "Let's get searching!"

That morning in the research room, the detective team worked right through until lunchtime without a break. By midday, when it was time to leave the museum, they had found several of Mr Scully's railway station photos taken on the morning of the accident. And, just as Ms Nulgit had said, Boldy appeared in almost all of them. But there was one hugely disappointing problem: although the time on the station clock could be clearly seen in most of the photos, the signal wasn't visible.

"It's too high up!" wailed Ella. "It's out of shot!"

"In *every* photo!" echoed Daisy.

"I'm over railway stations," groaned Kenji, "and now we have to spend our afternoon at one."

"I forgot we were going to visit the historic railway park this afternoon," sighed Ella, as Mr Snell appeared in the doorway of the research room.

"Ready, team?" he said. "Time to wrap up the investigation for now – the bus is waiting for you."

Chapter 12

"Click!"

The historic railway park was on the edge of town, and it had a real steam train called Betty that gave actual rides. Mr Kim, the park's tour guide, met everyone at the gates.

"We have four kilometres of railway track here," he explained, as he led the class to the platform of the historic railway station. "Our steam train, Betty, will take you around the track twice. Of course, our driver will obey all the signals our station master gives her, so don't be surprised if you have a stop on your way!"

At the word "signals", Ella's ears pricked up.

"Betty will arrive at the station in twenty minutes," continued Mr Kim. "Before you board, let me give you a tour of the station."

Mr Kim led the class into the station building and showed them the Morse code machine, which was used to send messages in the days before there were telephones. There was an old black stove in one corner of the station, a little bed with a knitted rug on it, and a wide wooden desk that Mr Kim said the station master would sit at when he wasn't needed outside.

"How did the station master control the signal?" asked Ella.

"He used a lever," said Mr Kim. "Many stations had levers inside the station building or in a special building called a signal box. Some small stations had their signal lever on the platform."

Ella looked around for anything that looked like a lever. "This station must have its signal lever on the platform," she said.

"Excellent observation!" said Mr Kim. "Let's go outside and I'll show you all how it works."

Ella wasn't quite sure why, but she felt it was very important to focus on what Mr Kim was about to show them. She wished she was closer to Daisy and Kenji, so she could tell them to concentrate, too, but they were at the back of the group.

On the platform, as the class gathered round a large shiny metal lever, Ella made sure she was standing right beside Mr Kim.

"When the lever is in this direction," he said, pointing to it, "the signal, which you can see a little further down the track, is horizontal, which means 'stop'."

Everyone looked down the track at the signal.

"Who would like to change the signal's position by pulling the lever into a new position?" asked Mr Kim.

Ella's hand shot up, and she was chosen. She grabbed the handle of the lever with both hands, and pulled it towards her. It slid into position with a satisfying, well-oiled thud. Further along the line, the signal fell into the vertical "go" position with a loud click. And, as it did so, something in Ella's brain went "click", too, and she realised that the detective team was much closer to solving the mystery surrounding the train accident.

Ella wished she could talk to Daisy and Kenji right away, but it would have to wait because, with a hiss, a creak and a huge rumble, Betty was slowly approaching the station in a cloud of steam.

That evening, when the class was back at School Lodge, Ella at last had an opportunity to talk to Kenji and Daisy. When she told them what she'd realised, and how it could help them solve the mystery of what *really* caused the train accident, they couldn't wait to get back to the museum to check their photos all over again.

"Please, please let Canvas Town station have its signal lever on the platform, too," said Daisy, as she, Ella and Kenji all crossed their fingers for good luck.

Chapter 13

Piecing It All Together

The next morning, Ella was so nervous that she gobbled down her breakfast without tasting it. Daisy and Kenji looked nervous, too. But, once they reached the museum and were in the research room, everyone's attention was firmly fixed on the photos.

"Yes!" said Kenji, who was holding the magnifying glass. "Look! There it is – thc signal lever *is* on the platform!"

Ella reached for a piece of paper. "Right," she said. "We have five of Mr Scully's photos taken on the morning of the train accident. In three of them, we can see the station clock, but not the signal."

Ella pointed to the lever. “However, we now know the position the signal lever is pointing in when the signal is set to ‘stop’ and when it’s set to ‘go’. So as long as we can see the *lever* in the photo, it doesn’t matter if we can’t see the signal itself!”

“Kenji,” said Daisy, “can you please take another look at the clock in each of the three photos where it’s visible, and tell us the time you see on it? I also want you to identify which way the lever is pointing, in each of those photos.”

Slowly and carefully, Kenji looked through the magnifying glass and relayed the information to Ella, who wrote it down. When he had finished, Ella could barely believe her eyes.

“At 10:15 am on the day of the accident, the position of the signal lever shows that the signal was set to ‘stop’,” she said. “That’s *after* Mr Brown would have left to go to his gold claim at 10 am! And at 10:35 am, the signal was *still* set to ‘stop’.”

“However,” said Daisy, looking over Ella’s shoulder, “at 10:50 am, the position of the signal lever shows the signal was set to ‘go’. How can that be?”

“Maybe Mr Brown came back and changed the signal because he thought it really should have been set to ‘go’,” said Kenji.

"No way!" said Ella. "He was the station master. He would have known what he was doing!"

"Some kids could have changed the signal for a joke," said Daisy. "A joke that went seriously wrong."

"No," said Ella. "That can't be right. The accident was on a Tuesday. I remember reading that in a newspaper article. All the school-age kids in Canvas Town would have been at school at that time of the morning."

"Good thinking," said Kenji.

"Unless …" said Ella, slowly. "Unless it wasn't a *person* who changed the signal at all!"

"Huh?" asked Kenji and Daisy at the same time.

But Ella was already reaching for the remaining photos, and as she studied them with the magnifying glass, she slowly began nodding her head.

"We're ready to begin making our display," she said to Daisy and Kenji. "But instead of starting from scratch, I have a better idea."

Chapter 14

The Detective Team Presents

For the rest of the time they had left at the museum, the detective team worked at top speed. Whenever Mr Snell or Ms Nulgit checked in to see how they were going, Ella, Daisy and Kenji quietly put an arm over their work so it couldn't be seen. By lunchtime on Friday, they were finished, but Mr Snell was concerned.

"Where's your display?" he asked, as everyone else in the class was putting the final touches to theirs, and covering them with sheets to keep them hidden until presentation time.

"We're going to put it up bit by bit, as we present the results of our investigation," said Ella.

"That sounds rather mysterious," said Mr Snell. "I hope you know what you're doing."

"We do!" said Kenji.

On Friday afternoon, Ella was surprised to see that several parents had driven to the city to watch the class's museum display presentations. Among them were Ella's mum and Nan! As Ella, Daisy and Kenji stood up to present, Ms Nulgit introduced them as "the detective team", and Mum and Nan waved.

Daisy opened the presentation by explaining the story behind the museum's gold mining display, and why the life-sized cardboard cut-out of Danny looked so sad and worried. She then said that having your dad go to prison would make anyone sad, but that it would be even worse if you knew your dad was innocent. As she spoke, Daisy reached under a sheet lying on the floor beside her, and held up a life-sized photo of Danny Brown's smiling face.

"We found this photo of Danny in the Canvas Town School records," she said. "We want Danny to look like this in the museum's gold mining display, because we can prove that his dad, Mr Brown the station master, really *was* innocent. We know he didn't cause the train accident that got him sent to prison."

Next, Kenji stood up and explained how signal levers worked on old railway stations. He said that, by looking at their position, it was possible to tell if a train signal was set to "stop" or "go".

"You don't actually have to see the signal to know!" he said.

Ella looked over at Ms Nulgit, who was listening intently to what Kenji had to say.

Finally, Kenji held up his magnifying glass, and explained how much more you could see in a photo when you looked through one of these "amazing old-fashioned devices".

"You can even tell the time on the Canvas Town railway station clock!" he said.

From under the sheet on the floor, Kenji took out a cardboard clock that showed 10:15 am, and a large poster with a diagram of how a signal lever worked.

"We found a bunch of photos of the Canvas Town railway station that were all taken on the day of the train accident," said Kenji. "The signal can't be seen in them, but the signal lever can be. In one important photo, the railway station clock says 10:15 am – that's after the time Mr Brown, the station master, would have left the station to go to his gold claim. In the same photo, the signal lever shows the station's signal was set to 'stop'."

Ella heard Ms Nulgit gasp, and when she looked over at her, she saw that Ms Nulgit had her hand over her mouth in surprise.

"But in another photo, taken just a short time later on the same day," continued Kenji, "the station clock says 10:50 am, and the signal box shows that the signal was set to 'go'!" He paused, and looked at the eager faces peering back at him. "Now, it's over to Ella, who will explain who, or should I say *what*, changed the signal and caused the train accident."

Chapter 15

Ella Explains

Ella stood in Kenji's place in front of the audience. From the back of the group, Mr Snell, who was also standing, gave her a thumbs up, and Ella took a deep breath. She then spoke about Boldy, the Canvas Town bull. She even made everyone laugh when she told them how she had read newspaper reports of Boldy coming out of the bush and chasing the Canvas Town grocer's cart along the road. There was a gasp when she said that the bull liked to chase children on their way to school.

"Boldy loved scratching his head and his back by rubbing against anything that was hard," said Ella. She told the story of how Boldy sometimes sent rocks rolling downhill towards the miners' tents, and everyone gasped again.

"We also know that Boldy liked to rub his back against the station's signal lever," explained Ella. "That's because we have a photo of him doing exactly that on the morning of the train accident – at precisely 10:45 am. That's just five minutes before we *know* the signal was set to 'go'."

From her seat in front of Mum and Nan, Ms Nulgit began nodding her head very slowly, as if she had a hunch about what Ella was going to say next.

"Boldy was big and strong," continued Ella. "He was far stronger than an adult. So, even though we can't see the signal lever in the photo (because Boldy is in the way, scratching himself on it), we know that it must have been Boldy who knocked the signal lever into the 'go' position."

From the back of the group, Mr Snell began clapping. Mum and Nan joined in, followed by everyone else. Ms Nulgit got to her feet, and walked to the front to stand beside Ella.

"Would it be okay if we added our photos and diagrams to the Canvas Town gold mining display?" Ella asked her. "We have some double-sided tape on the back of them."

"Be my guests, detectives," said Ms Nulgit, leading the way over to the display, with the audience following. "And congratulations on your team's research. I still don't know quite what gave you the idea to start investigating the crash in the first place, but I'm glad you did!"

It was only then that Ella realised she couldn't remember the last time Danny had spoken to her. With everything that had happened, it seemed like forever ago!

As Ella carefully cut out the copy they'd made of the school photo of Danny's smiling face and stuck it over the worried face on the cardboard cut-out, she asked herself again if she really had heard his voice. Or, if it was just a feeling inside her that had made her imagine that Danny had asked for her help.

Whatever it was, Ella decided as she was helping to pack away the tables and chairs later, Danny had helped her, too. Because of him, she'd taught herself to be better at focusing, just as Nan had done when she'd worked on her see-saw project. And not only on reading and writing; Ella had learnt to study photos closely, too – and how to concentrate when someone, like Mr Kim, was explaining something important. *And* she'd given a presentation without her mind wandering and making her forget what it was that she wanted to say. Ella felt sure she'd be able to focus on a book better at RED time, too, just as long as it was an interesting one. In fact, she might even ask Mr Snell if he had any detective stories she could read!

As she followed her classmates out of the city history hall, Ella looked back, half expecting that Danny might have something to say. But the cardboard cut-out, with its new, smiling face, was completely silent.

"Thanks," whispered Ella. "Thanks for everything, Danny!"